# Grave Gossip

BRIAN PATTEN

London
UNWIN PAPERBACKS

Boston          Sydney

First published in Unwin Paperbacks 1979
Reprinted 1983

This book is copyright under the Berne Convention. All rights are reserved. Apart from any fair dealing for the purpose of private study, research, criticism or review, as permitted under the Copyright Act, 1956, no part of this publication may be reproduced, stored in a retrieval system, or transmitted, in any form or by any means, electronic, electrical, chemical, mechanical, optical, photocopying, recording or otherwise, without the prior permission of the copyright owner. Enquiries should be sent to the publishers at the undermentioned address:

UNWIN® PAPERBACKS
40 Museum Street, London WC1A 1LU

© Brian Patten 1979

**British Library Cataloguing in Publication Data**

Patten, Brian
  Grave gossip.
  I. Title
  821'.9'14      PR6066.A86G/


  ISBN 0-04-821044-7
  ISBN 0-04-821041-2 Pbk

LINCOLNSHIRE
COUNTY COUNCIL

821

Typeset in 10 on 12 point Univers by V & M Graphics, Aylesbury
and printed in Great Britain
by Biddles Ltd, Guildford, Surrey

*In Memory*
*of Heinz Henghes*

Some of these poems have previously appeared in a number of magazines, including *New Departures, Aquarius,* and *The Fanatic*. Several have been published in a limited edition by Bertram Rota Ltd. Mostly the poems first found a public at poetry readings, and my thanks are due to the people who arranged the readings, and the many people who have attended them.

# CONTENTS

## THE WRONG NUMBER

One night I went through the telephone book name by name.
   I moved in alphabetical order through London
Plundering living-rooms, basements, attics,
   Brothels and embassies.
I phoned florists' shops and mortuaries,
   Politicians and criminals with a flair for crime;
At midnight I phoned butchers and haunted them with strange
      bleatings,
   I phoned prisons and zoos simultaneously,
I phoned eminent surgeons at exactly the wrong moment.
   Before I was half-way through the phone book
My finger was numb and bloody.
   Not satisfied with the answers I tried again.
Moving frantically from A to Z needing confirmation
   That I was not alone
I phoned grand arsonists who lived in the suburbs
   And rode bicycles made out of flames.
No doubt my calls disturbed people on their deathbeds,
   Their death rattles drowned by the constant ringing of
      telephones!
No doubt the various angels who stood beside them
   Thought me a complete nuisance.
I *was* a complete nuisance.
   I worried jealous husbands to distraction
And put various Casanovas off their stroke
   And woke couples drugged on love.

I kept the entire London telephone system busy,
    Darting from phone booth to phone booth
The Metropolitan phone-squad always one call behind me.
    I sallied forth dressed in loneliness and paranoia —
The Phantom Connection.
    Moving from shadow to shadow,
Rushing from phone booth to phone booth till finally
    I sought out a forgotten number and dialled it.
A voice crackling with despair answered.
    I recognised my own voice and had nothing to say to it.


## I STUDIED TELEPHONES CONSTANTLY


So I studied telephones constantly.
I wrote great and learned papers on the meaning of telephones.
I wondered what the last dispatch rider thought
galloping past the telephone wires, his body full of stale arrows.
I wondered what it would have been like
if Caesar had had a telephone.

I thought of nothing but telephones.
Night after night I invented numbers.
I placed trunk-calls to non-existent cities.
Jesus! I received so many weird replies.

I wondered if the dead would like a telephone.
Perhaps we should plant phones in graves so that the dead
might hold endless conversations
gulping in the warm earth.

Telegrams and telephones,
and not an ounce of flesh between them
only so much pain.

I began to consider them my enemy.
I joined underground movements dedicated to their overthrowal.
I vowed absurd vows,
I sacrificed daisies.
My hands were bloody with pollen.

I can imagine the night when waking from a nervous sleep
you find the telephone has dragged itself up the stairs one
                                                    at a time
and sits mewing,
the electronic pet waiting for its bowl of words.

    *

*Hello! Hello!*
*It's the evening phone-in show!*
*You've an abscess on the heart?*
*A tumour on the soul?*
*You're sleepless with grief?*
*You're in pain, you feel insane?*
*Neglected? Rejected?*
*You feel like a freak,*
*You feel bleak?*
*Lost your wife last week?*

*You're alone? Dying on your own?*
*Cancer crawls up the spine?*
*Well, fine!*
*Don't worry, don't care.*
*I'm on the air!*
*I'm DJ Despair,*
*I reek of the right answers!*

＊

It is so far from the beginning of telephones.

I thought of how it felt to be connected for the first time,
to be fifteen and uncertain while her mother says: 'Hang on'.
O the ecstasy of waiting for her to come down from her young room
    and answer!
The pinkness of telephones and the fragrance of telephones
    And the innocence and earnestness of telephones!
I'm sure those wires still cross paradise,
still fresh in the crushed ice of Yes!

Nothing in that conversation has changed.
She is still bemused at his agony as he struggles
    with the language of telephones.
O to be connected so!
Before shadows passed over the wires,
before trivia weighed them down,
when they trilled like sparrows and their voices were bright.

*

Where does God hide his telephone number?
No doubt the clergy have committed that number to memory.
Kneeling in their celestial phone booths
they phone him late at night while the lambs are suffering.
For the telephone is hard to resist
For it brings joy and misery without distinction
For the telephone is blameless
For it is a blessing to the hypochondriac
Both 'Help' and 'No' are in the word telephone.

And would it have made much difference
if Faustus had had a telephone?
Whose number was on Marilyn Monroe's lips the last time
                                                    she felt too tired?
What went wrong?
I was listening to the grave gossip.
Terror leaked from the mouth's pit.

In telephone exchanges the world over
The numbers are dying,
Vast morgues where the operators sleep-walk among the babble,
Where the ghost phones lament
for all the calls that went wrong.

Death owns everyone's telephone number.

And the night?
How many telephone numbers does the night possess?
The night has as many telephone numbers as stars.

## BLAKE'S PUREST DAUGHTER

'All things pass,
Love and mankind is grass'
    — Stevie Smith

Must she always walk with Death, must she?
I went out and asked the sky.
No, it said, no,
She'll do as I do, as I do.
I go on forever.

Must she always walk with Death, must she?
I went and asked the soil.
No, it said, no,
She'll do as I do, as I do.
I will nourish her forever.

Must she always walk with Death, must she?
I listened to the water.
No, it said, no.
She'll do as I do, as I do.
I will cleanse her forever.

Must she always walk with Death, must she?
No, said the fire,
She'll burn as I burn, as I burn.
She will be in brilliance forever.

O but I am not Death, said Death slyly,
I am only no longer living,
Only no longer knowing exorbitant grief.
Do not fear me, so many share me.

Stevie elemental
Free now of the personal,
Through sky and soil
And fire and water
Swim on, Blake's purest daughter!


## MONSTERS


He went on a journey to where he imagined
the need for journeys would have ended.
Much he saw and would have liked to have owned
was guarded by monsters.
It didn't surprise him. Yet that he had conjured them himself,
out of fear, out of absurd jealousies,
was unknown to him.
No wiser from that journey all he learned
was how best to destroy monsters.
Many have vanished, but listen —
much of what they guarded and that he wanted
has vanished with them.

# BURNING GENIUS

He fell in love with a lady violinist,
It was absurd the lengths he went to to win her affection.
He gave up his job in the Civil Service.
He followed her from concert hall to concert hall,
bought every available biography of Beethoven,
learnt German fluently,
brooded over the exact nature of inhuman suffering,
but all to no avail —

Day and night she sat in her attic room,
she sat playing day and night,
    oblivious of him,
and of even the sparrows that perched on her skylight mistaking
        her music for food.

To impress her, he began to study music in earnest.
Soon he was dismissing Vivaldi and praising Wagner.
He wrote concertos in his spare time,
wrote operas about doomed astronauts and about monsters who,
    when kissed,
became even more furious and ugly.
He wrote eight symphonies taking care to leave several
                                                unfinished,
It was exhausting.
And he found no time to return to that attic room.

In fact, he grew old and utterly famous.

And when asked to what he owed
his burning genius,
he shrugged and said little,

but his mind gaped back until he saw before him
the image of a tiny room,
and perched on the skylight the timid
   skeletons of sparrows still listened on.


## ONE SENTENCE ABOUT BEAUTY


When something vanished from her face,
When something banished its first light
It left a puzzle there,
And I wanted to go to her and say,
'It is all imagining and will change,'
But that would have been too much a lie,
For beauty does reach some kind of height
And those who hunger for her now tomorrow might
Have a less keen appetite.

## DRUNK

An interpretation of Baudelaire's prose poem,
The Drunken Song


People are sober as cemetery stones!
They should be drunk,
We should all be drunk!
Look, it's nearly night time and the sober news
Comes dribbling out of television sets —
It should be drunken news,
If only it were drunken news!
Only festivals to report and the sombre death
                                        of one ancient daisy.
It's time to get drunk, surely it's time?
Little else matters;
Sober the years twist you up,
Sober the days crawl by ugly and hunched and your soul—
   it becomes like a stick insect!


I've spent so much time in the company of sober and
                                        respectable men,
And I learned how each sober thought is an obstacle laid
between us and paradise.
We need to wash their words away,
we need to be drunk, to dance in the certainty
that drunkenness is right.


So come on, let's get drunk,
let's instigate something!
Let's get drunk on whatever we want—
on songs, on sex, on dancing,
on tulip juice or meditations,
it doesn't matter what—
but no soberness, not that!
It's obscene!

When everything you deluded yourself you wanted has gone
you can get drunk on the loss,
when you've rid yourself of the need for those things back
then you will be light,
you will be truly drunk.

For everything not tied down is drunk—
boats and balloons, aeroplanes and stars—
all drunk.
And the morning steams with hangovers,
and the clouds are giddy
and beneath them swallows swoop, drunk,
and flowers stagger about on their stems
drunk on the wind.

Everything in Heaven's too drunk to remember hell.

And the best monsters are drunken monsters,
trembling and dreaming of beanstalks
too high for sober Jack to climb,
and the best tightrope walkers are drunken tightrope walkers,
a bottle in each hand they stagger above the net made
    of the audience's wish for them to fall.

Drunk, I've navigated my way home by the blurry stars,
I've been drunk on the future's possibilities
and drunk on its certainties,
and on all its improbabilities I've been so drunk
that logic finally surrendered.

So come on
no matter what time it is
no matter where it is
in the room you hate
in the green ditch bloated with spring,

beside the river that flows
with its million little tributaries
into a million little graves,
it doesn't matter—
it's time to get drunk.

If one night of oblivion can wash away
all the petty heartache then fine,
reach for that ancient medicine.

And if you wake from drunkenness
don't think too much about it,
don't stop to think.
Don't bother asking clocks what time it is,
don't bother asking anything that escapes from time
what time it is,
for it will tell you as it runs,
leap-frogging over all obstacles,
Why idiot, don't you know? It's time to get drunk!
Time not to be the prisoner of boredom

or cemetery stones!

Be drunk on what you want,
Be drunk on anything, anything at all
but please—
Understand the true meaning of drunkenness!

# A FEW QUESTIONS ABOUT ROMEO

And what if Romeo,
lying in that chapel in Verona,
miserable and spotty, at odds with everything,
what if he'd had a revelation from which
Juliet was absent?
What if, just before darkness settled
the arguments between most things,
through a gap in the walls he'd seen
a garden exploding,
and the pink shadow of blossom
shivering on stones?
What if,
unromantic as it seems,
her mouth, eyes, cheeks and breasts suddenly became
ornaments on a frame
common as any girl's?

Could he still have drunk that potion had he known
without her the world still glowed
and love was not confined
in one shape alone?

From the prison the weary imagine
all living things inhabit
how could either
have not wished to escape?
Poor Romeo, poor Juliet, poor human race!

## THE COMMON DENOMINATOR
Or, The Ground-Floor Tenant's Only Poem


*What on earth are you about?*
I've hardly stopped to work that one out.
I don't know why—
I'm about blood of course, and love,
About sex and death,
About fear and half-hearted tenderness—
At a clouded intellect I've hurled
All the clichéd answers in the world,
But mostly it's the day to day
Trivia of getting by
That drains the energy to wonder why
the question's even asked.
*Who are you? Where from? And why?*
Like a plastic Buddha I have sat
Besuited under mindless trees,
And thinking of the mindless lilies in their fields
I've mused a bit and then
Been confused a bit and then
Still left unsolved such mysteries.
Don't get me wrong—
I'm not convinced there is such a thing
As a wholly complacent man,
All face a private terror now and then,
And nightly through most bedroom walls
Something uninvited crawls.
*Who? What? Whither? Why?*
I do not know nor very often care,
And as I walk, averagely mindless through the sunny air,
I leave the questions hanging there,
And try my best not to despair;
And try my best not to despair.

# IN THE HIGH-RISE ALICE DREAMS OF WONDERLAND

She received a parcel through the post.
It had everything she wanted inside it.
Sometimes when she touched it
a planet-sized man would come to the door
and say exactly the right kind of thing.
The parcel kept her happy.
Provided all she needed.
Her children blossomed,
grew fat and pink and healthy.
The high-rise in which she lived shrank,
became a neat house—
a swing on the lawn, a driveway, etc.

A bill for the parcel arrived on Monday
On Tuesday came a reminder.
On Wednesday came a solicitor's letter.
On Thursday came a court order.
On Friday the jury gave a verdict.
On Saturday the parcel was taken.
Most days
Alice can be seen in the high-rise,
mouth twisted, weeping.

# A BIRD-BRAINED VIEW OF POWER

The bird is paranoiac.
It thinks the leaves are trash piled up around it.
It sings as if it were a criminal,
feeding the silence and then retreating.

Headlights roaming through the trees
Support its delusions.

In the darkness the drab bird broods:
'Surely all this singing is keeping
Important people awake?
Rising from an irritated bed
Tomorrow a Minister will declare war
On some unfortunate province,
And somewhere a tired businessman will make
   The wrong decision and cities
Will be thrown into chaos.'

   In distant mansions
The guard-dogs multiply like rabbits.
God's bigots stalk one another,
Bull-necked or starry-eyed,
They deal in baby-jam.

In the branches the drab bird sings.
Absurd and clichéd as it sounds
In the branches a bird is singing,
singing with mindless persistency
   The one song it knows.
From the night and from antiquity
It has dragged up a single jewel.

24

Somewhere in a city, in a city
Cordoned by fear
A fistful of feathers believes
Its song has summoned up demons.
It listens to the wail of sirens.

Headlights roaming through the trees
Support its delusions.


## PROCLAMATION FROM THE NEW
## MINISTRY OF CULTURE


A festival is to be held during which
A competition is to be held during which
Work that exalts the free spirit of this land
May be submitted.
The judges can be chosen from among yourselves
The honours to be awarded are numerous,
The prizes to be awarded are numerous.
You may write or paint exactly what you wish,
You may say exactly what you wish
About the free spirit of this land.

Work in bad taste will be disqualified.
Anonymous entries will be ferreted out.
Those who do not enter will be considered
Enemies of the free spirit of this land.

From now on the festival is to be an annual event.

## TRAPPED (1)
### A Melodrama

*After a night of drunken revelry our hero makes a discovery*

O what a terrible fate it must be
To be trapped all night inside the Poetry Society.
To be alone with a vase of grey flowers,
leather chairs and bookshelves stuffed
With other people's sorrows.

*He considers his Fate*

What a terrible fate for the industrious poet
To stand at the third floor window writing
!qleH on the glass, having nothing but pigeons
To witness his plight.

The door is jammed,
No matter how much he pushes it it won't open,
For on the other side someone has cunningly
        stacked
A pile of dead mayflies.

*He broods upon his mentors and realises taste and cunning are called for*

And what an awful decision it must be
Choosing what volume to throw through the
        glass.
Would Keats land more gently than Donne?
Would the inspired crowd howl for Blake?
O surely to throw McGonagal out
Would be the safest bet!

*Devoid of inspiration, he doubts the significance of grey flowers*

Trapped thus, what can the poor poet write?
The vase of grey flowers alone
Is unworthy of a poem.
The view from the window is too daunting a
        prospect
And his own sufferings
Are rather minimal.

*Illustrious ghosts gossip among the bookcases*

Would Shakespeare have suffocated him with
        beauty?
Would Coleridge have overwhelmed him with
        opium saying
'Hey kid, sniff this, it's ancient dope!'
Would poor John Clare
have threatened him with a pitchfork?
Left him in a madhouse homesick for visions?
Would he have drowned in Gray's Elegy,
Picked Wordsworth's daffodils and sold
the lot in the market-place?

*Our hero is rescued and the poem concluded*

All night he will wander fretting in the gloomy
        rooms of the Poetry Society,
Until in the morning dear John Betjeman rises
        above
    the roof of Marlborough Railway Station
        disguised as the sun,
And a thousand librarians,
all heavily disguised as Philip Larkin,
Come, jangling the keys to his absurd dilemma.

**TRAPPED (2)**
In The Bowels Of Cornell University, Or:
The True Confessions Of A Manuscript Sniffer

Deep down in the library vaults protected by verse-loving
Dobermann Pinschers I stumbled upon the literary remains of
William Wordsworth. What paradise deep in those pristine
catacombs to fondle the remains of Emily Dickinson! To run cold
and licentious eyes over the liquid prose of Virginia Woolf, to
stoke, sick with passion, a bundle of mildewed manuscripts from a
Northamptonshire asylum.

And what joy it was to tour those vaults where, by the stench of
the still fresh air, I could tell I was among the more recent
acquisitions of Cornell!

It was here I came upon the newly interred left eye of Robert
Lowell, an eye that still blinked out in serious astonishment. And
here in a special vault reserved for new mythologies I saw an exact
replica of a Belsize Park gas oven, and in a jar next to it, preserved
in brine, the tarry lungs of Auden wheezed on in exasperation.
Here too I unearthed the mummified corpse of some long dead
beauty; a tag around the throat informed me, 'About this creature
much great poetry was written.'

And among the limbs and bloodless bits of human junk I
discovered the greatest of all treasures: the decomposed kidneys of
Dylan Thomas smuggled at great expense from a New York
morgue. Thus does poetry survive in Academia.

Might I suggest in future
the bodies of all dying authors are wrapped in their
                                            manuscripts and frozen
and preserved in zoos and funfairs
so that the student of literature
might study under more realistic conditions
the state of the battered and bartered and lovely human soul.

# CONVERSATION WITH A FAVOURITE ENEMY

At a dinner party in aid of some unsufferable event
I sit opposite my favourite enemy.
'How's the cabbage?' he smiles.
'Fine,' I say, 'How's your novels?'
Something nasty has started.
On the chicken casserole the hairs bristle.
On the hostess the hairs bristle.
She glances down the dinner table
her eyes eloquent as politicians'.
'Do you find the dumplings to your liking?' she asks,
'Do you find them juicy?'
'Fine,' I say, 'How's your daughter?'
She chokes on the melon.
After supper he's back again,
Wits sharpened on the brandy.
He folds his napkin into the shape of a bird,
'Can you make this sing?' he gloats,
'Would you say it's exactly poetry?'
Ah, but I'm lucky this evening!
In a tree outside a nightingale burst into fragments.
It flings a shrapnel of song against the window.
My enemy ducks, but far too slowly.
It is not always like this.
My enemies are more articulate,
The nightingale, utterly unreliable.

## GHOST-CULTURE

The Minister kneeling on the floor hunched over
the home politics page slobbering
pink fingers counting the column inches given
his ghost-written speech on how best
to decapitate the landscape
the hostess
well-feathered house stuffed with finery
the little poet rasping out the tough sonnet
the morose social worker wearing
last year's most expensive fashion
as some kind of penance
the charming young publisher
the charmed financier
the nouveau poor sucking up the atmosphere
the black writer of revolutionary pamphlets
the priest holding forth from the plush armchair
on man's fall from paradise
glib mimic living in light's echo
the neat journalists
the purveyors of wound-cream
the high-class gossip merchants
the sour novelists
the past and present beauties
the landlords of Bedlam
the manipulators of ghost-culture
all history's goblins
agile among the contradictions
were stunned into an embarrassed silence
when from his pocket the guest of honour
produced a few crumpled and unexplained petals
and wept with exhaustion.

**PIPE DREAM**

If I could choose the hour in which
Death chooses me,
And the way in which
It will make its arbitrary choice,
I can think of nothing better than
To fall asleep near midnight in a boat
As it enters a new port,
In a boat
With a clarity of stars above
And below it,
And all around me
Bright music and voices laughing in
A language not known to me.
I'd like to go that way,
Tired and glad,
With all my future before me,
Hungry still for the fat
And visible globe.

**WAVES**

And the one throwing the lifebelt,
Even he needs help at times,
Stranded on the beach,
Terrified of the waves.

# THE CRITICS' CHORUS
Or, What The Poem Lacked

'How he got to the point of thinking this sort of thing
was a poem is a good and appalling question . . .'

-Donald Davie

Of course they were right:
The poem lacked a certain tightness,
Its inventions were chaotic.

*In the bleak farmhouse Rimbaud*
*remembering the jewelled spider webs,*
*The smoking pond, the banished sideshows.*

Of course they were right:
The poems were not fit to be taken seriously,
Mere candyfloss, the efforts of a stablehand.

*In Rome coughing up the rose-shaped phlegm*
*Keats taking the final opiate,*
*the nightingale suddenly obsolete.*

Of course they were right:
He could have found all he wrote
In the dustbins he emptied.

*Where's Hyatt now?*
*Still drinking the blind wine?*
*Ghost-junk still flowing in ghost-veins?*

Of course they were right:
So much of what she wrote was doggerel,
mere child's play.

*In a London suburb Stevie,*
*Blake's grandchild,*
*fingering a rosary made of starlight.*

Of course they were right:
In all the poems something went astray,
Something not quite at home in their world,
something lost.

It was something to do with what the poem lacked
saved it from oblivion,
a hunger nothing to do with the correct idiom
In which to express itself

but a need to eat a fruit far off
from the safe orchard,
reached by no easy pathway
or route already mapped.

# THE RIGHT MASK

One night a poem came to a poet.
From now on, it said, you must wear a mask.
What kind of mask? asked the poet.
A rose mask, said the poem.
I've used it already, said the poet,
I've exhausted it.
Then wear the mask that's made
Of the nightingale's song, use that mask.
But it's an old mask, said the poet,
It's all used up.
Nonsense! said the poem, it is the perfect mask.
Nevertheless, try on the God mask—
Now that mask illuminates Heaven.
But it is a tired mask, said the poet,
And the stars crawl about in it like ants.
Then try on the troubadour's mask, or the singer's mask,
Try on all the popular masks.
I have, said the poet, but they fit so awkwardly.
Now the poem was getting impatient,
It stamped its foot like a child. It screamed,
Then try on your own face!
Try on the one mask that terrifies you,
The mask no one else could possibly use,
The mask only you can wear out!
He tore at his face till it bled.
This mask? he asked, this mask?
Yes, said the poem, why not?
But he was tired even of that mask.
He had lived too long with it.
He tried to separate himself from it.
Its scream was muffled, it wept,
It tried to be lyrical.

It wriggled into his eyes and mouth,
Into his blood it wriggled.
The next day his friends did not recognise him,
The mask was utterly transparent.
Now it's the right mask, said the poem,
The right mask.


## STARING AT THE CROWD


I saw the skeleton in everyone
And noticed how it walked in them,
And some, unconscious that Grinning Jack
Abided his time inside their flesh
Stared back, and wondered what I saw.
The way they dressed, a boil on a face,
Their vanities were small and obvious—
Women wore their coldest masks and men
Looked elsewhere and thought perhaps
I was some friend they'd dropped.
But I did not know them well enough to say
It's Grinning Jack I see today,
Not your beauty or your ugliness,
Nor how fresh you seem, nor how obvious
The chemical decay,
But the skeleton that every man
Ignores as calmly as he can,
Who'll kiss us on the cheek and blow
The floss of temporary things away.
It's Grinning Jack I see today,
And once seen he'll never go away.

# SONG OF THE GRATEFUL CHAR

I'll scrub the doorstep till it blinds you,
I'll polish the candlesticks till they burn,
I'll crawl across the carpet
And suck up all your dirt.

Though the cast-off clothes you gave me
Are much too grand to wear
I'll don them in the bedroom,
And no doubt I'll weep there.

I'll wash the shit from your toilet,
The stiffness from your sheets.
Madam, thank you for employment.
Can I come again next week?

'Sweetheart.' said the banker's wife,
'I too know of despair,
I think about it often
In my house in Eaton Square.'

'Sweetheart,' said the doctor,
'I've no advice today.'
Pain had made him indifferent.
He turned his head away.

Among a pile of nightmares
I heard a woman scream.
'Hush,' said the psychiatrist,
'It is a common dream.'

There are many kinds of poverty,
My mother knows them well.
She sits and counts them in a tenement
A mile or so from hell.


## NOTE FROM
## THE LABORATORY ASSISTANT'S NOTEBOOK


The Dodo came back.
It took off its hat.
It took off its overcoat.
It took off its dark glasses and
put them in its suit pocket.
It looked exhausted.

I made sure the doors were locked.
I turned off several lights.
I got the blood from the fridge
and injected it.

Next I sneaked into the garden and buried
a manuscript containing
The History of Genetic Possibilities.
I washed my fingerprints from things.

I took a Bible down from the shelf.
Opening it at Genesis I sat waiting.

Outside, people not from the neighbourhood
were asking questions.

## BRER RABBIT IN THE MARKET PLACE

Today they've been feeding Brer Rabbit.
They've coaxed him down from the hillside,
hidden the furgloves, the rabbit-feet,
the coats worn by ugly women have for today at least
been banned from the market.

'It's Kindness to Rabbits Week,' they explain,
'Skinbag, let's fatten you!
Everyone will want to know you,
Everyone will want to stroke you.
Imagine the comfort!
Imagine the bunnies you could get into!'

Today they are being charitable to Brer Rabbit.
They feed him with lettuce and carrots,
offer fine plates artistically set with flowers,
they show him the most comfortable hutches,
the plastic burrows, the new, grass-free hillsides.
Brer Rabbit doesn't mind.
He eats and says nothing.
He is the one rabbit who will never stay,
who will never grow quite fat enough.

He will be away by nightfall,
when under the glittering kerosene lamps
the fat bunnies are hung and skewered
and all manner of freaks parade between
the meat stalls and the apples.

## BRER RABBIT'S HOWLER

Brer Rabbit goes to the ball dressed as a dandy.
He feels good this evening.
Magnanimous towards all creatures, he cannot understand
why the dancers shy away from him.
What social misdemeanour is it now
that they stiffen at?
He's eaten the lice.
He's washed off the stench of burrows.
The myxomatosis scabs are healed.
What's left to complain about?
He dances to whatever tune's available,
the fox trot, the tango;
his green suit becomes him,
in his lapel
the baby's foot looks charming.


## BRER RABBIT AND THE SPARROW

Brer Rabbit watches a sparrow.
It jumps up and down, a furious little sparrow.
Its beady eyes stare at him.
It snarls from behind leaves,
on the branches it sharpens its beak.
If only it could get at him
it would gobble him up,
this sparrow, light as a sunbeam,
as temporary as vision.

39

# BRER RABBIT AND THE RAINBOW

Brer Rabbit arrives at the rainbow's ending,
stunned, frightened of its brilliance.
He dips a paw into the colours expecting much to happen,
but nothing changes. He tries to drink the colours,
but again nothing.
With a blade of grass he saws through the spectrum,
he tackles each separate colour,
each glowing beam is gone through, its points examined.
And still nothing is understood,
the reason for its brilliance eludes him.

Brer Rabbit arrives at the rainbow's ending.
He digs into the ground,
the turf smells of morning, it befriends him.
He ruffles the soil, digs down exposing
intricate insects, peculiar stones, but still
no bits of gold reward him.
And while Brer Rabbit digs,
while he hunts befuddled through a maze of tree-roots
above ground clouds are appearing.
Deeper and deeper digs the rabbit.
Abandoning light abandoning leaf abandoning treasure

## BRER RABBIT'S REVENGE

So Brer Rabbit re-enters the burrow.
All day he's been in the world of fantasy,
but now below the drenched allotment
he is at home again.

Through the walls of his burrow rain leaks,
the tunnels turn liquid;
his fur mud-soaked he screams
his hatred of make-believe.

All day he's been bunnying about—
smiling benevolently with the toy shop dummies,
wandering through the nursery
all winsome and innocent.

Now that above ground the children sleep
cocooned in love for him
something drops away and sweetness
is no longer bearable.

Soon enough those children will grow old.
Brer Rabbit climbs into his shroud.
He waits to haunt them.

# BRER RABBIT AND THE ANTS' BANQUET

Brer Rabbit sends out messages;
'All's finished here.
In the burrow memory falls away until
There is nothing to cling on to.'
He digs for some image, for some route back
To a time when company existed.
He comes up with nothing.
He watches how frost melts from the apples,
Thinks how the world might be empty, thinks
How old plagues might have settled.
'Once I breakfasted on roses,
I gossiped with tulips,
I invited friends home,
Got them drunk on the brilliant petals!
But then the clouds swarmed,
They sucked up colour. All went.
Blank poppies, small memories of redness.
Little rags, without essence.'
He sniffs the mist to trace a scent,
But there is no difference now
Between enemy and flower.
Daily his brain tightens.
On the leaves he has written his messages;
They darken then vanish.
From the dandelions he has unhooked his longings;
On the wind that changes pollen into dust
They drift, then vanish.
He sinks down the long burrow frightened.
Brer Rabbit changes.
He becomes the ants' banquet,
A focal-point for the flies' reunion.

Into the landscape his brown fur merges.
Soon without fear or shape he will run
Through tunnels of fern and campion,
Down trackways that have for centuries led
From door to green door
Brer Rabbit will be flowing.


## JOHN POOLE'S BULLYING THE ANGELS


John Poole's bullying the angels.
In Paradise the cherubs are shivering with fear,
When his big nasty shadow stomps past
their curls droop.

What's John Poole doing in Paradise,
Smashed on the queer stuff?
How the hell did he get in?
Well, he was that kind of person.

He scared policemen
And loved rabbits and battered women
and loved rabbits.

Maybe that's how he got in.
He loved rabbits more than the cherubs.
He said so, strolling towards Paradise
in a threatening sort of way.

43

## FROGS IN THE WOOD

How good it would be to be lost again,
Night falling on the compass and the map
Turning to improbable flames,
Bright ashes going out in the ponds.

And how good it would be
To stand bewildered in a strange wood
Where you are the loudest thing,
Your heart making a deafening noise.

And how strange when your fear of being lost has subsided
To stand listening to the frogs holding
Their arguments in the streams,
Condemning the barbarous herons.

And how right it is
To shrug off real and invented grief
As of no importance
To this moment of your life,

When being lost seems
So much more like being found,
And you find all that is lost
Is what weighed you down.

# THE MULE'S FAVOURITE DREAM

When the mule sings the birds will fall silent.
From among them they will choose a messenger.
It will fly to the court of the Emperor
And bowing with much decorum
Will complain bitterly.

And the Emperor, who had long ago banished all cages,
Who until that moment had been astonished
By the birds' flight and by their singing,
Will throw open the windows and listening
Will detect in the mule's song
Some flaw of which he is particularly fond,

And he will say to the bird, 'O stupid thing!
Let the mule sing,
For there has come about a need of change,
There is a hunger now
For different things.'

This is the mule's favourite dream.
It's his own invention.
Deep in his brain's warren it blossoms.

# THE LAST GIFT

H.H. 'What's the story about?'
B.P. 'About a mouse that gets eaten by an eagle.'
H.H. 'Poor mouse.'
B.P. 'No, the mouse becomes part of the eagle.'
H.H. 'Lucky mouse. Perhaps I'll be that lucky.'


Perhaps next time he will be
a musician playing in a hall in which
a few children fidget and dream
while the crowd regrets
what cannot help but pass.
Or perhaps he will be something a snowdrift's buried
and that's not found again,
or the contradiction of blossom
on a stunted apple-tree.

   Perhaps,
but all I know for certain
is that already some friends are in their graves,
and for them the world is no longer fixed
in its stubborn details.

Astonished in moments of clarity to realise
how all that surrounds me has passed
again and again through death,
I still strut without understanding
between an entrance of skin and an exit of soil.

It is too much to expect he will come back
in the same form,
molecule by sweet molecule reassembled.

When the grave pushes him back up
into the blood or the tongue of a sparrow,
when he becomes the scent of foxglove,
becomes fish or glow-worm,
when as a mole he nuzzles his way up
eating worms that once budded inside him,
it's too much to expect that I'll still be around.

I'll not be here when he comes back
as a moth with no memory of flames.

It is a dubious honour getting to know the dead,
knowing them on more intimate terms,
friends who come and go in what at the last moment
seems hardly a moment.
And now as one by dreamless one they are dropped
into the never distant, dreamless grave,
as individual memory fades
and eye-bewildering light is put aside,
we grow more baffled by this last
gift of the days they are denied.


## HOPEFUL

Alone, tired, exhausted even
by what had not yet happened,
passing a cemetery on the outskirts of London I saw
an angel dip its hand into a grave
and pull out a fistful of cherry-blossom.

## ONE REASON FOR SYMPATHY

I rescued a bee from a web last night.
It had been there several hours,
Numbed by the cold it could hardly fight
A spider half its size, one programmed
To string a web across the fattest flowers
And transform the pollen into bait.
My sympathy I know now was misplaced,
It had found the right time in which to die.
I saved it while light sank into grass
And trees swelled to claim their space;
I saved it in a time of surface peace.
Next morning as I watched the broken web gather light
Seeing it ruined in the grass I understood
That I had done more harm than good,
And I felt confused by that act
Of egocentric tenderness.
I called it love at first, then care,
Then simple curiosity,
But there was a starker reason for such sympathy.
It is that one day I too will be caught out in the cold,
And finding terror in there being no help at hand
Will remember how once I tried to save a bee—
Though I hope the same mess is not made of me.

# GOING BACK AND GOING ON

Trying to get back before night hid the way
And the path through Sharpham Wood was lost
I still found time to stop, and stopping found
A different path shining through the undergrowth.
It was real enough—
A sun that had been too high to light
The underside of leaves had sunk,
And ground level rays had lit
The tiny roots of things just begun.

Just now begun! To think on this half-way through
                                   what time is left!
Among the dead and glittering brambles on the path
The miracle is obstinate.
There is no 'going back', no wholly repeatable route,
No rearranging time or relationships; no stopping
Skin from flaking like a salmon's flesh.
Yet no end of celebration need come about,
No need to say,
'Such and such a thing is done and gone'—
The mistake is in the words, and going back
Is just another way of going on.

## SOMETHING NEVER LOST

There is a place where the raspberries burn
And the fat sparrows snore in peace;
Where apples have no fear of teeth,
And a tongue not used to dust
Sings of something never lost;
It is a place not far away.
It takes a lot of trust to reach,
And a spell only love can teach.


## ADVICE FROM THE ORIGINAL GATECRASHER
## TO THE RECENTLY DEAD

If you arrive outside Paradise and find
entrance is by invitation only and that anyway
from the ledger your name is missing,

do not despair.

At the back of Paradise
in the huge wall that surrounds that place
is a small door;

God and all his angels have forgotten it.

If something goes wrong
and Heaven ignores you,

if what you are is paraded before you and mocked,
do not despair,

you have got too near
for your schemes to be abandoned.

If you are told to go away,
to Hell,
to the blankness already experienced,

you simply sneak round the wall
to the small door at the back of Heaven,

you give it a bit of a push,
and wriggling like a snake
you squeeze yourself in.

And if you ever get hungry no doubt
somewhere you will find an apple tree,
and fruit to share quite generously.

# THE PURPOSE IS ECSTASY

But if you enter without rapture or without
such hopes as make hoping actual,
you might as well not enter—

'Now' is weighed down by 'ago',
sight's overloaded and the smell
of earth burdened by memory.

What use dragging the body and all
its loose desires and its ghost-connections
through days wounded by doubting,

the purpose is ecstasy —

believe in it, undo the mischief
night's wardens have created.

This is the message I leave myself—
Yet so hard to rise out the trap
of befuddled longings!

Habit hauls in its net,
bulging with Death's cartographers.

## FRIENDS
For Liz Kylle


I met them in bars and in railway stations
and I met them in borrowed rooms
and at bright gatherings,
    and often enough
I met them with misgivings and doubts,
and misinterpreted what they said
or did not understand at all, or understood so well
no explanations seemed needed.

And still, for all this,
I kept on losing them.
    And changes took place and things
that had seemed extraordinary and out of reach
became life's most obvious gifts,
and the world slowed down, and I began
to meet them less and less.

Then I learned how the exodus from this place is not
                                            scheduled—
at times the young leave before the old
    and the old
are left gaping at their fortune.

Looking through a book containing
the names they have abandoned
I realise that as from today
I haven't fingers enough to count
the graves in which they are exiled.

## ASSEMBLING A PRAYER

So many were spreading darkness as if it were light,
they were broadcasting their sicknesses and their ghosts
hoping they would go, but needing them;
they were digging up the mummified gods
and pulling at their spines to make them gibber.

   One of Death's little camp followers
I went along with them, chattering sombrely,
my back to the sunlight, arse about face,
   my sight permanently fixed in important shadows.

There came a time I believed the future mapped,
that everything was arranged —
except for the daily trivia there seemed
       nothing left to plan,
and though it was still a mystery what route I'd take
  and with what cool or lush flesh I'd wake,
I believed what I was was in the blood,
that for good or bad
the chemistry of incident and memory was fixed.

   Then I learnt
how to throw away the tragic books,
I began ignoring the philosophies that wilted
                   at the grave's edge;
the smell of grass became revelation enough.

I needed a new philosophy, a new god, a bright god,
        a light, sun-splashed god.
A god that can gobble up the sickness and the ghosts,
a god that can blow grief away
        as if grief were a feather.

Out of such things I have began to assemble a prayer.

## Other Brian Patten Poetry Collections

### NOTES TO THE HURRYING MAN

'A magic ability to turn radiant imagination loose in the cities and streets and lonely bedrooms of modern living.'

*The Times*

### THE IRRELEVANT SONG

'His . . . marked sensitivity and eye for the unusual . . . puts Patten among our best young writers.'

*The Guardian*

### VANISHING TRICK

'Patten has emerged with this new collection into a fully matured talent, taking on the intricacies of love and beauty with a totally new approach, new for him and contemporary poetry. He is the master poet of his genre, the only one continually and successfully to "ring true".'

*Tribune*

### LITTLE JOHNNY'S CONFESSION

'His poems . . . are newspaper captions that need no photographs . . . loving creatures which will survive all newspapers.'

*Adrian Mitchell*

'A remarkable portrait of the bewilderment of an urbanized generation.'

*Jerome Cushman – Library Journal USA*

BRANSTON SCHOOL AND
COMMUNITY COLLEGE